DRAWBRIDGE

Story and photographs by Richard Latta

Richard C. Owen Publishers, Inc.
Katonah, New York

The   car   stops.

The gate is down.

Up goes the drawbridge.

A boat passes through.

Down comes the drawbridge.

Up goes the gate.

And across the bridge we go.